THIS BOOK BELONGS TO:
BRAINERD

To our children, that they may always have a home in the holler.

ABOUT THIS BOOK

The illustrations for this book were done in Adobe Illustrator.
The text was set in Bookman Old Style Regular.
This book was edited by Mary-Kate Gaudet.
The production was supervised by Erika Schwartz
and the production editor was Barbara Bakowksi.

Additional production work by Zane Peterson
Special thanks to Jennifer Jacobs and Lyndy Butler

Little, Brown and Company

Hachette Book Group
1290 Avenue of the Americas, New York, NY 10019
Visit our website at lb-kids.com

Little, Brown and Company is a division of Hachette Book Group, Inc.
The Little, Brown name and logo are trademarks of Hachette Book Group, Inc.
The publisher is not responsible for websites (or their content)
that are not owned by the publisher.

First Edition: November 2014

Library of Congress Cataloging-in-Publication Data
Jacobs, Parker, illustrator.
Welcome to Goon Holler / by Parker Jacobs and Christian Jacobs.
pages cm
Summary: Tooba, a lonely, timid, and always hungry bigfoot, stumbles upon Goon Holler,
where Dosie takes him to a Goon Scout pancake breakfast and helps him make new friends.
ISBN 978-0-316-40550-8 (paper over board) — ISBN 978-0-316-40548-5 (library edition ebook)
[1. Friendship—Fiction. 2. Bashfulness—Fiction. 3. Sasquatch—Fiction. 4. Scouting (Youth activity)—Fiction.]
I. Jacobs, Christian, 1972– . II. Title.
PZ7.J152517Wel 2014
[E]—dc23
2014004201

10 9 8 7 6 5 4 3 2 1
SC
Printed in China

Welcome to GOON HOLLER

Written by Parker Jacobs and Christian Jacobs
Illustrated by Parker Jacobs

Little, Brown and Company

New York Boston

Toobaloth C. Grassfoot
was hungry.

He tromped through the
woods as he always did,
looking for something to eat,
with no one to talk to but
his grumbly tummy.

"Well, Tummy, maybe if I climb up this tree, I can find some fresh bark to chew on," Toobaloth said.

Startled by an angry possum,
Toobaloth fell from the tree!

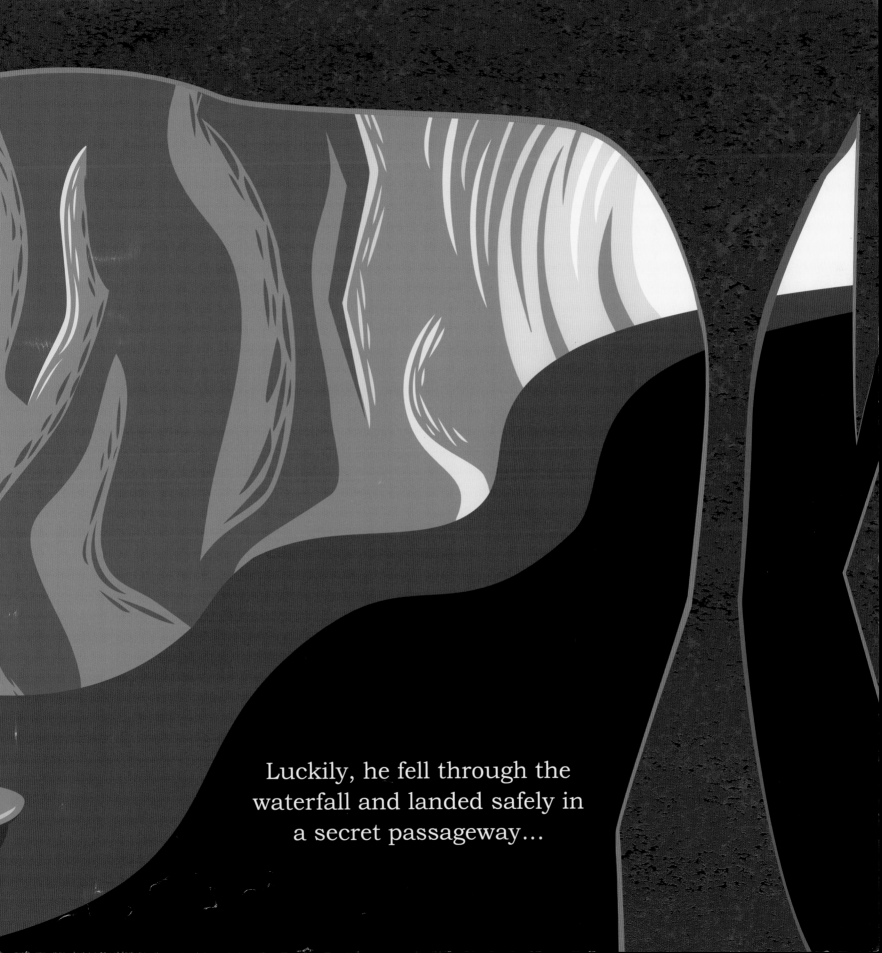

Luckily, he fell through the waterfall and landed safely in a secret passageway...

...which led to a bright and wonderful place
that Toobaloth had never seen before!
It looked delicious! "Food!" he exclaimed.

"Excuse me, mister. Why are you eating bark from an apple tree?" said a little girl who seemed to pop out of nowhere.

"Uh-oh. Were you going to eat this bark? I'm sorry. I was just so hungry," he said.

"Of course not, silly! I was just askin'! My name's Dosie. What's your name?"

"My name is Tooba—"

But before he could finish, he was startled by something moving in the distance.

"Oh, that's just a little Goon Scout," she said.
"He's probably heading over to the Goon Holler
Goon Scout pancake breakfast."

"I have no idea what you said," replied Tooba.
"What is a Goon Scout? What is a holler?
What is a pancake?"

"Tee-hee! Just come with me," giggled Dosie,
pulling him along, "and no more tree bark
for you. That's just gross!"

So together they followed the little
Goon Scout up the path to the place
she called Goon Holler.

As they came to the middle of a village swarming with more of these furry little goon creatures, Tooba could not believe what he was seeing! Goons of all shapes and sizes were hustling and bustling in and out of their curious little homes.

Tooba followed Dosie to the lodge and they both got right in line for breakfast!

The helpful Goon Scouts served Tooba a hot plate
of bacon, eggs, and a tall stack of fresh pancakes.
For the first time in his life, he began to feel like
he was among friends.

At the table,
Tooba took
his first bite.
The pancakes
tasted so
wonderful,
he felt like
he was flying
in pancake
heaven!

His tummy agreed.

"Tooba, I need to warn you about something," said Dosie.

Suddenly, **VROOOOOOM!**

A goon in a hot rod plowed right through the picnic area.
He was chasing a whole rafter of turkeys and spewing
mud, turkey feathers, and food everywhere.

Everyone but Tooba dropped what they were doing
to join in the wild-turkey chase. He was shocked!

Then Tooba noticed that over by the pancake griddle, a fire was starting to spread!

"**FIRE!**
There's a fire!"
he cried.

But the goons could not see
they were in trouble.

"Dosie," cried Tooba, "why don't they understand?"

"Well, the only thing they DO understand is FUN," said Dosie as they tried to stop the fire by themselves.

It was the word
"FUN"
that gave Tooba
a swell idea!

He dumped water on the nearest goon
and hollered two words:

"WATER FIGHT!"

Instantly, the turkey chase turned into a water fight. Water balloons flew, buckets splashed, and before the goons even noticed, the fire was out. Tooba and Dosie had saved the day!

That night, Tooba found a nearby cave to sleep in.
As he drifted off to sleep, he decided he'd make
Goon Holler his permanent home.

And he never
had to eat
bark again.

GOON HOLLER
DEPUTY
FIRE
CHIEF
TOOBA

THE END